LOTTIE LUNA

AND THE FANG FAIRY

First published in Great Britain
by HarperCollins *Children's Books* in 2020
HarperCollins *Children's Books* is a division of HarperCollins*Publishers* Ltd,
HarperCollins Publishers
1 London Bridge Street
London SE1 9GF

The HarperCollins website address is
www.harpercollins.co.uk

1

ISBN 978-0-00-834304-0

A CIP catalogue record for this title is available from the British Library.

Printed and bound in England by CPI Group (UK) Ltd, Croydon CR0 4YY

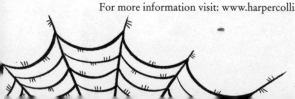

LOTTIE LUNA
AND THE FANG FAIRY

VIVIAN FRENCH

Illustrated by Nathan Reed

HarperCollins *Children's Books*

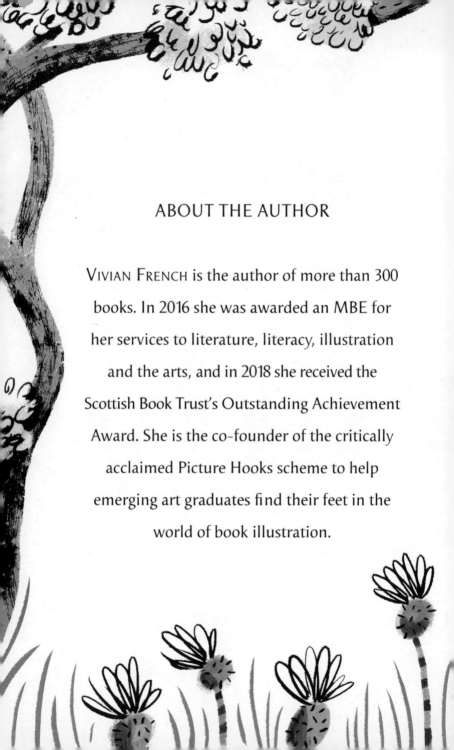

ABOUT THE AUTHOR

VIVIAN FRENCH is the author of more than 300
books. In 2016 she was awarded an MBE for
her services to literature, literacy, illustration
and the arts, and in 2018 she received the
Scottish Book Trust's Outstanding Achievement
Award. She is the co-founder of the critically
acclaimed Picture Hooks scheme to help
emerging art graduates find their feet in the
world of book illustration.

To Jenny down the stair,

with love

CHAPTER ONE

'**Absolutely** not!' King Lupo banged the milk jug down on the breakfast table, and frowned. 'My daughter, Princess Lottie Luna, going camping? Sleeping in a tent? Cooking food outside in the open? No, no, NO! That is NOT suitable. Not at all!'

Lottie gulped. She and all her friends at Shadow Academy had been looking forward to the school trip for weeks. She couldn't be the only one left behind! What would she do? The idea of sitting all by herself in an empty classroom for three whole days made her feel terrible.

'But Pa . . . Ma said I could go! Everyone in my class is going! We've got loads and loads of things planned - we're going on a hike to look at rocks, and we're going to collect wildflowers, and we're going to—'

'I told you, Lottie!' King Lupo's eyebrows bristled. 'It's not suitable. A princess must always be dignified!'

'Yeah. Dead right.' Lottie's big

brother, Boris, took his elbows off the table and sat up straight. 'You've got be more royal, Lottie. Like me.'

Lottie ignored him, and turned to her mother. 'Ma! Tell Pa I've got to be allowed to go! PLEASE!'

Queen Mila sighed. 'Your father worries an awful lot about royal behaviour, Lottie.'

'That's right.' The king began to butter his toast. 'A king should always be kingly, and a princess should always be – erm – princessy!'

A cunning thought made Lottie try a different approach. 'But, Pa – don't you think I ought to learn to be dignified in every situation? I mean . . . isn't it good to learn to be princessy even on a hike?'

'That's a very sensible point, dear.' The queen looked at the king. 'I did tell Lottie that she could go, Lupo. It'll be a whole new experience for her. After all, you've never had the opportunity to be kingly in a tent. You shouldn't take the chance away from Lottie!'

The king paused over his toast, and Lottie held her breath. Would he change his mind? At last he said, 'You might be right, Mila. Lottie – I have decided you should go!'

'Oh, dearest, lovely, gorgeous Pa!' Lottie flung her arms round her father and hugged him. 'Thank you so, SO much!'

The king beamed at her. 'Just remember, though – you're to be a princess at all times!'

'Oh, I will, Pa – I will!' Lottie promised. 'And

I'll tell you all about it when I get back, but now
I'm going to pack!' And she bounced out of the
breakfast room.

As Lottie hurried along the
dusty passage towards her
room, she was humming to
herself. Jaws, her pet bat, was
flying above her head, and her
moonstone necklace was shining brightly.

She's happy now, Jaws told himself, and he
looped a celebratory loop.

It was easy to tell how Lottie was feeling: her
necklace changed according to her mood. If she
was happy, it shone brightly, but if she was bored,
it was grey, and if she was sad or worried it was

so dull it looked like a pebble.

The necklace had been given
to her on the night she was born;
not only had the moon been full,
but there had been a lunar eclipse as
well and, as a result, Lottie was a unique little
werewolf with very special powers. She had
extraordinary eyesight, could run like the wind,
was far stronger than her older brother – and her
hearing was at least three times more acute than
that of her friends.

Lottie kept very quiet about her special powers,
however, especially at school. She desperately
wanted to be the same as everyone else – and she
never, ever told anyone she was a princess. Only
her two best friends, Wilf and Marjory, knew . . .
and they were sworn to secrecy.

'What else do I need, Jaws?' Lottie stared at the backpack on her bed. 'I've got loads of woolly jumpers, pyjamas, my washbag, toothbrush and toothpaste . . . oh, and a sleeping bag.'

Jaws flew a quick circle, dipped down and pointed a wing at something on the floor. Lottie looked round. 'Oh, YES! My walking boots! Thanks, Jaws.' She stuffed them on top of her pyjamas, and swung the backpack over her shoulder. 'Ooof! It's heavy! But at least I've got everything . . . I hope.'

She glanced at the clock on the wall, and gasped. 'Oh, no! I'm going to be late! And Mr Sprinter said he wouldn't wait for anyone! That's the trouble with teachers – they always want you to be on time!'

Dashing out of her bedroom, Lottie hurtled down the corridor and burst into the breakfast room. 'Bye, dearest Pa! Bye, lovely Ma! Bye, Boris! I'll see you in three days' time!' Catching sight of her father's expression, she hastily added, 'And yes! I'll be INCREDIBLY dignified and princessy!'

And then she was out of the door and running as fast as she could, Jaws squeaking encouragement above her head.

CHAPTER TWO

Lottie was only just in time. Wilf and Marjory were standing outside the school bus, arguing with Mr Sprinter, when Lottie came tearing towards them. They both cheered loudly.

'Sorry, Mr Sprinter,' Lottie panted. 'I'm really sorry!'

'You're very lucky you have such good friends, Lottie.' Mr Sprinter sounded cross. 'If they hadn't refused to get on the bus without you, we'd have left five minutes ago. Now hurry up and take your seats! We can't delay any longer.'

Lottie gave Wilf and Marjory a grateful smile as the three of them climbed on board. 'Thank you very, very much,' she said. 'Pa tried to stop me coming . . . it was awful!'

Agatha Claws, a tall girl with a long nose, sniffed. 'MY father always supports me whatever I do. He's bought me lots of boxes so I can bring interesting specimens home to study, and I've got a magnifying glass and three new notebooks.'

Wilf nudged Lottie as the bus roared away down

the road. 'Aggie's got twice as much luggage as any of us,' he whispered. 'Mr Sprinter nearly had a fit!'

Lottie tried not to giggle, but she wasn't entirely successful, and Aggie gave her a suspicious look. 'Are you laughing at me?'

'Of course not, Aggie.' Lottie tried to look nonchalant.

'I'm sure a magnifying glass will be really useful,' Marjory said quickly. 'Can we borrow it sometimes?'

Aggie gave a superior smile. 'I'll have to see. It cost a lot of money.'

Larry, one of the younger cubs, had been listening. 'I'm going to have some money soon! I got a wobbly tooth, and my mum says that when it comes out the fang fairy will take it away and give me a silver coin!'

The twins, Tod and Dubby, were sitting beside Larry, and they nudged each other and began to sing.

'Larry's got a wobbly tooth,
A wobbly tooth,
A wobbly tooth.
Larry's got a wobbly tooth –
A wobbly-gobbly, toothy-woothy tooth!'

'That's exciting,' Lottie said, and she

smiled at Larry. 'The fang fairy used to give me money too. Don't forget to put your tooth under your pillow so she can find it!'

'A wobbly tooth?' Mr Sprinter turned round and beamed at the little werewolf. 'That's exciting! Is it your first one?'

'Yes!' Larry bounced up and down in his seat. 'I never had a tooth come out before!'

'Then we'll have to celebrate,' Mr Sprinter

said. 'We'll have a special party for you . . .
a Tooth Party!'

Larry was thrilled. 'It's EVER so wobbly! I'm
sure it's going to pop out ever so soon!'

Aggie gave a dismissive sniff. 'What a silly fuss!
I didn't have a party when my first tooth came
out. I thought it was much too babyish!'

Tod and Dubby sniggered. 'Larry is a baby, a
baby, a baby—'

'Hush!' Lottie said. 'I think a Tooth Party's a
great idea. I had one when I was little, and so did
my brother.'

Larry suddenly looked anxious. 'The fairy will
be able to find me while I'm away at camp, won't
she?'

'Of course she will,' Lottie told him. 'The fang
fairy finds everyone everywhere.'

'That's right.' Marjory nodded. 'One of my teeth came out when I was staying with my auntie, and the fairy still came, even though I was miles away from home.'

'Huh!' Aggie snorted, and Lottie noticed there was a mean look in her eyes. 'Don't you know there'll be a different kind of fang fairy where we're going, Larry? The fairies in the country are much fiercer than the ones where we live!'

'Are they?' Larry looked anxious again, and Wilf frowned at Aggie.

'They're all the same,' he said firmly. 'Now, why don't we sing a song? What about, "We're all going on a jolly howlyday"?'

That made Larry laugh, and he, Tod and Dubby, and all the other little werewolves sang happily as the bus trundled over the hills and

15

deep into the Greater Growling Woods. Lottie,
Marjory and Wilf sang along too; only Aggie
didn't join in. She sat and stared out of the
window until they arrived at the clearing where a
group of tents was surrounded by tall, whispering
pine trees. As soon as the bus stopped, she
leaped to her feet and was the first one out, using
her elbows to push her way past the younger
werewolves.

Wilf rolled his eyes. 'Bet she's gone to bag the

best tent,' he said, and he was right. When Lottie
and Marjory went to look, they found Aggie had
arranged her piles of luggage in the tent nearest
the campfire . . . and there was no room inside for
anyone else.

'It's meant to be three to a tent, Aggie,' Mr
Sprinter told her. 'I thought you could share with
Lottie and Marjory.'

Aggie fluttered her eyelashes. 'Dear Mr
Sprinter! Please let me be on my own! I want

17

to make sure that I get plenty of sleep, so I'm all ready to help you – and Lottie and Marjory are sure to keep me awake with their chatting. Besides, Lottie's got her pet bat with her, and he'll flutter about all night.' She put her head on one side, and gave him a sickly-sweet smile. 'You can use all the specimen boxes that Daddy gave me.'

Mr Sprinter hesitated, and Wilf stepped forward. 'I can share with Lottie and Marjory. At least . . . as long as they don't mind?'

'I don't mind at all,' Marjory said, and Lottie grinned at him.

'Just as long as you don't snore!'

'Thank you, Wilf.' Mr Sprinter sounded relieved. 'Very well, Aggie. The tent is yours, and yours alone. Now let's get that campfire built!'

CHAPTER THREE

It didn't take long for Lottie, Marjory and Wilf to arrange their sleeping bags in a row in their tent. As soon as that was done, they hurried around, collecting sticks and fir cones from under the trees, while Mr Sprinter hauled over a couple of heavy logs from a pile that had been left ready beside the toilet block.

The campsite was often used by schools and a very elderly werewolf looked after it. He made sure there was always plenty of wood, and that it was kept tidy. The rest of the time he dozed in his

shed, and ate cheese-and-tomato sandwiches.

'We'll soon have a fine blaze,' Mr Sprinter said as Lottie and her classmates piled up the sticks and cones and dried leaves. 'We'll roast potatoes in the embers . . . and then we'll have hot chocolate!'

'With marshmallows?' Marjory asked hopefully, and Mr Sprinter nodded.

'Of course!'

Marjory sighed with pleasure, and Wilf grinned at her. 'Happy?'

'Oh, yes,' Marjory told him. 'Hot chocolate with marshmallows is my most favourite thing ever.'

Aggie stuck her nose in the air. 'I think that's very childish of you, Marjory.'

'No it's not.' Lottie rushed to defend her

friend. 'Anyway, if you don't like hot chocolate, can Marjory have yours?'

'I didn't say I didn't like it,' Aggie said. 'I just think it's a bit of a baby's drink.' And she tossed her head, and walked away.

Wilf watched her go, his eyebrows raised. 'She's in ever such a mean mood. What's upset her?'

Marjory shrugged. 'She's just being Aggie. Although she did seem furious when we made Mr Sprinter wait for Lottie. She kept muttering about favourites, and people who thought they could do exactly what they wanted.'

'Oh, dear.' Lottie looked guilty. 'I didn't mean to be late. I do hope she cheers up a bit!'

'Mr Sprinter says we're going to tell bedtime stories round the fire after supper,' Wilf said.

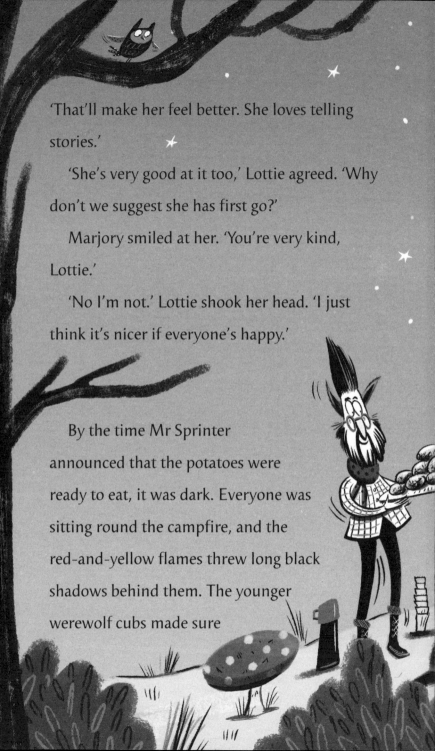

'That'll make her feel better. She loves telling stories.'

'She's very good at it too,' Lottie agreed. 'Why don't we suggest she has first go?'

Marjory smiled at her. 'You're very kind, Lottie.'

'No I'm not.' Lottie shook her head. 'I just think it's nicer if everyone's happy.'

By the time Mr Sprinter announced that the potatoes were ready to eat, it was dark. Everyone was sitting round the campfire, and the red-and-yellow flames threw long black shadows behind them. The younger werewolf cubs made sure they were sitting very close together, and Lottie nudged Marjory. 'Poor little things! They look a bit nervous!'

Lottie was right, but by the time the cubs had eaten a huge baked potato and drunk an enormous mug of hot chocolate heaped high with marshmallows they seemed much happier. They were giggling and pushing, and rolling each other over on the grass until Mr Sprinter clapped his hands.

'Time for a bedtime story! Who's going to go first?'

Lottie put up her hand. 'Please, Mr Sprinter – Aggie's a brilliant storyteller!'

Mr Sprinter turned to Aggie. 'Would you like to begin?'

'Of course, Mr Sprinter.' Aggie was delighted. 'I've got just the right story too!'

'Excellent.' The teacher settled back. 'Make yourselves comfortable, everyone – and Larry! Stop wriggling!'

'My story's especially for Larry,' Aggie said, and Lottie looked at her in alarm. What was she going to say? She had a nasty feeling that Aggie was hoping to scare the little cub.

'It's a story about the hideous fang fairy who lives in the Greater Growling Woods,' Aggie began. 'She's not like the fang fairy we have at home . . . the nice, kind fairy who leaves a silver coin under your pillow. The fairy in these woods has huge bulging eyes and long yellow fangs . . . and she creeps around at night, hunting for any little werewolf who might have a loose tooth . . . and then she tiptoes up to them and she SNATCHES the tooth—'

'No she doesn't!' Lottie jumped to her feet. 'She's just as lovely as the fang fairy at home!'

But she was too late. Larry was shaking, and his eyes were very wide. He stared at Aggie. 'Will she come and get me tonight?'

Before Aggie could answer, Lottie had run over to Larry and was hugging him. 'Don't worry,' she

said. 'It's just a story Aggie made up.' She glared
at Aggie. 'That's right, isn't it? You made it up!'

The mean look was back on Aggie's face. 'I
might have done,' she said, 'or I might not.'

Mr Sprinter gave a loud and hearty laugh.
'Nothing like a horror story when you're sitting
round a campfire! You weren't really scared, were
you, Larry? I'm sure you're much too big to be
frightened by Aggie's fairy tale.'

Larry's friends giggled, and Tod growled loudly
and tweaked Larry's arm. 'I'm a toothy-woothy
fang fairy, I am!'

Dubby sniggered. 'I'm a horrid, scary, hairy
fairy, and I'm on the hunt for Larry!'

The other little cubs fell about, howling with
laughter . . . all except Larry. He tried to laugh,
but Lottie saw that he was very pale. She put an

arm round his shoulders, gave him another hug and shook her head at the twins.

'Don't be mean, Tod and Dubby. They're only teasing you, Larry. Truly! Don't be scared!'

'That's right, Lottie!' Mr Sprinter laughed again. 'But let's have something more cheerful now. It's my turn, so I'm going to tell you about the flowers and butterflies that can be found here. Quite a few of them are very rare—'

'Just like the Greater Growling Fang Fairy,' Aggie interrupted.

Mr Sprinter looked annoyed. 'I think we've heard enough about that for now, thank you, Aggie.'

One of the other students put up her hand. 'Will we need butterfly nets?'

Mr Sprinter shook his head. 'I don't want you

to catch any butterflies. I want you to draw them.
That's what your notebooks are for – so you can
draw pictures of the things you see.'

Lottie, Wilf and Marjory gave each other a
high five. All three of them loved drawing; this
hike was going to be fun!

'Now listen very carefully.' Mr Sprinter was
suddenly serious. 'I do have something important

to tell you. When we're out tomorrow, I don't want any of you to go anywhere near the cliff on the other side of this hill. It's very dangerous indeed, and it would be terrible if one of you fell over the edge. Stay in groups of three or four, and keep well away!'

CHAPTER FOUR

Just as the campfire started to die down, another school bus arrived, and Lottie's teacher, Mrs Wilkolak, got out. She was followed by Mr Sprinter's wife. Mrs Sprinter was the cook at Shadow Academy, but she also ran the after-school nature club that Wilf went to every Tuesday. Everyone was delighted to see them; even Larry,

who had been very quiet all evening, gave Mrs
Wilkolak a hug.

'I got a wobbly tooth,' he whispered. 'Mrs
Wilkolak – will the fang fairy know where I am?'

Lottie overheard him. *He's still worrying*, she
thought, and she was about to tell him, yet again,
that what Aggie had said was a silly made-up
story when Mrs Wilkolak nodded.

'Don't you worry, Larry! The fang fairy can
always find you!'

'Oh.' Larry was so obviously disappointed that
she looked at him in surprise.

'Aren't you hoping to get a silver coin?' she
asked, but Larry didn't answer. He slipped away,
and Lottie saw him crawling into his tent. She
hurried after him, but when she peeped inside he
was curled up in his sleeping bag. Even though

31

his eyes were tightly shut, Lottie was certain he was awake, and she leaned forward.

'Larry? Larry – listen to me! You're absolutely safe! Marjory and Wilf and I are in the tent next to yours, so, if you feel in the least bit scared, just call!' She didn't want to tell Larry that her special powers gave her such incredibly acute hearing that she could hear a moth flapping its wings. Instead, she said, 'Don't worry. I'll hear you.'

The little wolf cub opened one eye. 'But what if you don't? What if Tod and Dubby tell me more scary stories? I don't like it when they do that.'

'Hey! I've had a brilliant idea!' Lottie's smile shone out. 'You can borrow Jaws to keep you company tonight! That would make you feel better, wouldn't it?'

Larry nodded, and gave a little sigh.

'Thank you. Night-night, Lottie.'

Lottie blew him a kiss. 'Sleep well!'

That night, Lottie lay awake for a long time, even though she could hear Larry, Tod and Dubby breathing peacefully in the tent next door. Marjory and Wilf were asleep within minutes of wriggling into their sleeping bags, but Lottie could hear hundreds of noises she had never been so close to before. Owls hooted in the distance, tiny animals rustled through the grass, the trees whispered to each other, and insects buzzed and fluttered. She could also hear Mr and Mrs Sprinter chatting to her teacher, Mrs Wilkolak, and she buried her head under her pillow. Having

extra-special hearing was sometimes a problem. Lottie did her best to avoid listening to things she shouldn't, but it wasn't always easy.

At last even the grown-ups had gone to bed. Lottie smiled to herself when Mr Sprinter begin to snore. Mrs Sprinter complained, and he stopped, but a moment later he started again, just more softly. Mrs Sprinter sighed heavily, and Lottie stifled a giggle. *I never knew Mr Sprinter snored*, she thought. *That's so funny!*

Gradually, she began to feel sleepy . . . but what was that?

Lottie sat bolt upright, and listened. Someone was tiptoeing towards her tent . . . she was sure of it.

'Wilf! Marjory!' She put out a hand and shook Marjory, but Marjory made a snuffling noise,

and her eyes stayed firmly shut. Wilf turned over with a grunt, but he didn't wake either. Lottie felt under her pillow for her torch, but then she remembered that it was at the bottom of her backpack and, before she could find it, the footsteps tiptoed away.

Maybe it was just one of the teachers checking on us? she thought, although she had a feeling that it wasn't. The steps had definitely sounded sneaky, as if whoever it was didn't want to be seen or heard.

Lottie yawned. I'll have a look for footprints in the morning, she decided as she snuggled down. And I'll tell Wilf and Marjory about it . . .

Her thoughts faded, and she was soon fast asleep.

35

'Wakey-wakey!'

It took Lottie a second to remember where she was. She rubbed her eyes and peered out of the tent. Mr Sprinter was banging a frying pan with a stick. Soon everyone was awake. The memory of the night before flooded into Lottie's mind, and she leaped out of her sleeping bag. She needed to look for clues.

She went outside. Yes! There were footprints very near her tent . . . but there were far more around Larry's. Whatever or whoever it was had circled it several times, and when Lottie looked more closely she gave a little gasp. Claws! There was no doubt about it. Those were claw marks.

'What are you looking at, Lottie?' Wilf was beside her.

'Shh . . .' Lottie put her finger to her lips,

37

and Wilf's eyes widened as she pointed to the prints. 'Something was outside last night,' she whispered. 'It was running round the outside of Larry's tent!'

'Ooooh! Are those claw marks?' Marjory was peering at them as well.

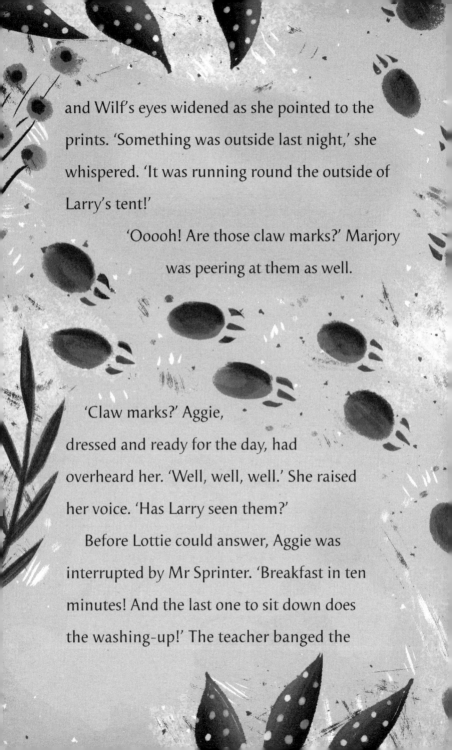

'Claw marks?' Aggie, dressed and ready for the day, had overheard her. 'Well, well, well.' She raised her voice. 'Has Larry seen them?'

Before Lottie could answer, Aggie was interrupted by Mr Sprinter. 'Breakfast in ten minutes! And the last one to sit down does the washing-up!' The teacher banged the

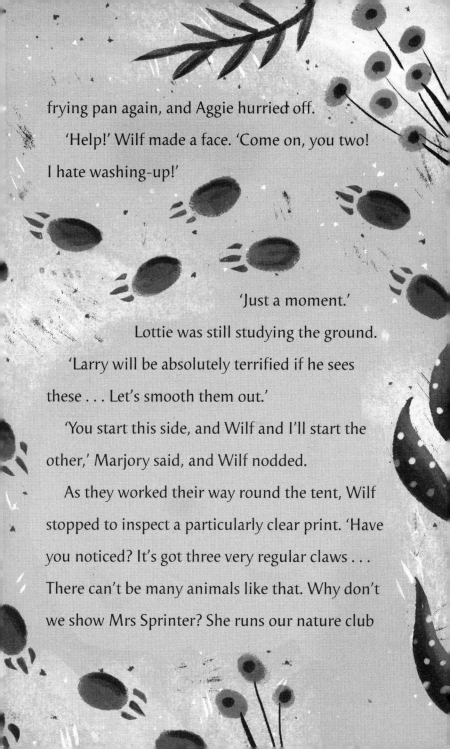

frying pan again, and Aggie hurried off.

'Help!' Wilf made a face. 'Come on, you two!
I hate washing-up!'

'Just a moment.'

Lottie was still studying the ground.

'Larry will be absolutely terrified if he sees
these . . . Let's smooth them out.'

'You start this side, and Wilf and I'll start the
other,' Marjory said, and Wilf nodded.

As they worked their way round the tent, Wilf
stopped to inspect a particularly clear print. 'Have
you noticed? It's got three very regular claws . . .
There can't be many animals like that. Why don't
we show Mrs Sprinter? She runs our nature club

and she'll probably say it's some harmless little rabbit or something, and then Larry will be fine.'

'The marks look too big for a rabbit, though,' Marjory said, and she shivered. 'It is a bit creepy, isn't it?'

'That's why Larry mustn't see the prints,' Lottie said firmly. 'If it happens again, then we'll show Mrs Sprinter.' And she went on smoothing the ground. As she did so, her necklace swung out from under her scarf, and she noticed that it was very dull. *Oh, dear*, she thought. I *must be more worried than I imagined.*

Jaws came squeezing out of the tent, and flapped up on to her shoulder. He saw Lottie's necklace, and squeaked anxiously.

'It's all right,' Lottie told him. 'Someone's just trying to scare Larry, and I'm going to find out who!'

CHAPTER FIVE

As soon as all traces of the night-time prowler had been cleared away, Wilf, Lottie and Marjory rushed to get washed and dressed . . . but they were still the last to join the breakfast queue.

'It looks like we'll definitely be doing the washing-up,' Wilf said. 'Oh, well . . . I suppose somebody has to do it.'

'I'll help you, Wilf!' Larry and his friends were just in front. 'I'm very good at drying-up. I hardly ever break things!'

Wilf grinned at him. 'Thanks. We'll get it

done in no time if we all work together.'

'That's cheating!' Aggie looked down her long nose. 'Larry wasn't last – you were!' She gave the little werewolf cub a sideways glance. 'How's your tooth?'

Larry opened his mouth wide to show her. 'Still wobbly.'

'Guess what!' Aggie's eyes gleamed. 'I heard the fang fairy wandering about last night. I expect she was looking for you!'

Tod and Dubby stared at her, and Larry began to tremble. 'Ooooh! Did you see her?'

Aggie shook her head. 'I just heard her. But there are claw marks outside your tent. Lottie saw them, didn't you, Lottie?'

Lottie paused for a moment. She didn't want to tell a fib, but she also didn't want to scare

Larry. She shook her head. 'I didn't see any claw marks when I went past just now.'

Tod and Dubby giggled, and Tod pretended to scratch at his twin. 'Hairy, scary fairies have ever such sharp claws!' he said.

'Hairy, hairy, ever so scary!' Dubby sang. 'Larry's scared of hairy fairies!'

At once Tod joined in. 'Hairy Larry's scared of fairies!'

'That's right, Tod,' Aggie said, and Lottie frowned.

'There aren't any hairy, scary fairies. Don't tease him, Aggie!'

As Larry looked from Lottie to Aggie, wondering who to believe, Mrs Wilkolak called to them from behind the serving table. 'Hurry up, you stragglers! Don't you want your breakfast?'

'Oh, yes, please!' Wilf was enthusiastic. 'Come on, Larry – and you too, Tod and Dubby . . . hurry up and get your porridge.'

Aggie looked suspiciously at Lottie, but she didn't say anything. She tossed her head, and went off to her tent, muttering under her breath.

'Phew!' Lottie linked her arm through Marjory's. 'I didn't tell a lie, did I?'

Marjory smiled at her. 'No. I thought you were very clever actually.'

Lottie rubbed her nose thoughtfully. 'Why's Aggie being so mean to Larry? He's only little.'

'I don't know.' Marjory shrugged. 'She loves being the centre of attention . . . Maybe she's cross because Mr Sprinter said there'd be a special party when Larry's tooth came out?'

'Perhaps we should keep an eye on him,' Lottie

suggested, and Marjory nodded her agreement.

'Those twins aren't helping,' she said. 'They
seem determined to make things worse.'

Wilf heard her, and laughed. 'Tod and Dubby?
They think everything's funny. My gran is best
friends with their mum, and Gran says they drive
the poor woman mad. They've always been like
that . . . singing songs, and playing tricks, and
generally being a nuisance.'

'Well, I wish they wouldn't,' Marjory said.
'Come on, Lottie. Let's get our breakfast.'

'And then it's washing-up time . . .' said Wilf.

The washing-up didn't take too long. Mrs
Wilkolak insisted on helping, and Larry did his
best to help with the drying-up. Marjory made

sure he only dried up the tin mugs and plates,
so it didn't matter when he dropped them.

'Butterfingers!' Wilf said cheerfully as Larry
dropped his third mug, but Lottie hushed
him. She thought that Larry was
looking worried again.

'Are you still thinking about the fang fairy?'
she asked.

The werewolf cub shook his head. 'I knows
what I got to do. I going to be fine, I is. That

horrid old fang fairy isn't going to catch me!
Not never!' And he sounded so certain that
Lottie was reassured.

'That's good,' she told him, and she picked up
the mug and handed it to Wilf.

'Here – can you wash this one again?'

Wilf took the mug in an absent-minded way
and put it down beside him. He was studying
a fork and frowning. 'That's odd,' he said. 'It's
all muddy!'

Marjory laughed. 'There's mud everywhere
here! Just look at your boots!'

But Lottie inspected the fork in Wilf's
hand, and guessed what he was
thinking. The fork was a large
one, and it had three prongs . . .
and the marks outside Larry's

tent had looked like they'd been made by a three-clawed animal.

Had someone being playing tricks? Could they have used the fork to deliberately try to scare the werewolf cub?

By the time they had put the last cup away, Mr Sprinter was organising the groups for the High Hill hike. After everyone had been given a notebook, a water bottle, a whistle and a handful of snacks, the teacher folded his arms.

'Keep in your groups,' he said, 'and don't leave the path. There's only one route up to the top of the hill, so you can't get lost. Mrs Sprinter will be waiting for you up there with a picnic ... so it'll be well worth the walk! Mrs Wilkolak will

be following behind you, and I'll be running up and down to check that everyone's all right. But, if you're worried by anything, just blow your whistle.'

Mrs Wilkolak nodded. 'And I want you to find at least ten different plants, or animals, or birds. You can draw pictures in your notebooks, or you can write a description of what you've seen.'

'Wow!' Wilf's eyes shone. 'One of Mrs Sprinter's picnics? That's brilliant!'

Aggie had reappeared, carrying an enormous backpack, and she gave Wilf her most superior stare. 'I'm sure to be the best. Last year I collected lots and lots of interesting flowers; nobody had as many as I did.'

'But, Aggie – some of those flowers were very rare! Please don't pick any this year,' Mrs

Wilkolak warned her. 'You can collect leaves . . . but if you pick flowers they can't grow the seeds for next year's plants.'

Aggie tossed her head. 'I know all about rare flowers. I've got a book in my backpack!'

'Good,' Mrs Wilkolak said, but Lottie wasn't entirely convinced that Aggie knew what she was talking about.

When Mr Sprinter read out the list of groups, Lottie, Wilf and Marjory were delighted to find they were all together. They weren't quite so happy when Aggie was included, but they smiled at her, even though she scowled as she came to join them.

'Actually, I'd rather go on my own,' she said.

'You'll just hold me back . . . After all, I've done this hike twice before.'

'Marjory and I have done it before as well,' Wilf pointed out. 'And I don't see why you think we'll hold you back. Lottie can run faster than any of us!'

Aggie looked at him scornfully. 'It's not about speed, Wilf. It's about studying nature, and finding interesting specimens.'

Marjory, always the peacemaker, could see that Wilf was going to carry on arguing, so she stepped between them. 'Let's see how we get on,' she said. 'I'm sure we can each do our own thing, and still keep together.'

'Maybe,' Aggie said, and she managed a faint smile.

CHAPTER SIX

Larry, Tod, Dubby and the rest of their classmates were running and jumping along the path in front of Lottie and her friends,

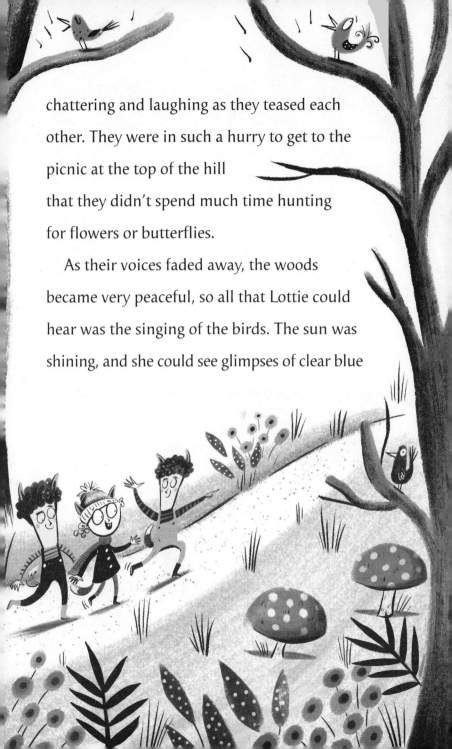

chattering and laughing as they teased each other. They were in such a hurry to get to the picnic at the top of the hill that they didn't spend much time hunting for flowers or butterflies.

As their voices faded away, the woods became very peaceful, so all that Lottie could hear was the singing of the birds. The sun was shining, and she could see glimpses of clear blue sky in between the topmost branches of the trees where the leaves were quivering in the faint breeze. She sighed happily, and began to look around her.

Marjory and Wilf were already drawing in their notebooks, and Lottie was just in time to see the whisk of a tail as a squirrel disappeared round a tree trunk. Aggie was studying a mushroom. As Lottie watched, she opened up her backpack and took out a little box to put it in. She saw Lottie looking, and made a face at her.

'Don't you dare draw it in your notebook,' she said. 'I saw it first!'

'I wasn't going to,' Lottie told her. 'I'm going to draw a squirrel . . . and a blackbird . . . and an owl!'

54

Aggie looked suspicious. 'You can't have seen an owl. Owls come out at night, not during the day.'

'Up there.' Lottie pointed, and then realised that it was only because of her extraordinary eyesight that she could see the tawny owl peering out of the dark hole at the top of an old oak tree. She hesitated, wondering if her advantage made the competition unfair. Deciding that it might, she said, 'I could be mistaken.'

'You are.' Aggie swung her bag on to her back. 'And I'm going on ahead.'

'But Mr Sprinter said we had to stay together,' Marjory objected.

'Oooooh!' Aggie's tone was mocking. 'What a goody-goody two shoes! I won't go far.' And, before anyone could say anything else, she had marched away.

55

Lottie, Marjory and Wilf stared at each other. 'What do we do now?' Wilf asked.

'I suppose we should tell Mrs Wilkolak,' Marjory said, but she sounded doubtful.

Lottie shook her head. 'Then we'd be telltales. Why don't we just follow on behind her? After all, we'll all be on the same path . . . and, if we catch her up, she can't complain.'

'Sounds good to me,' Wilf said.

'And me,' agreed Marjory.

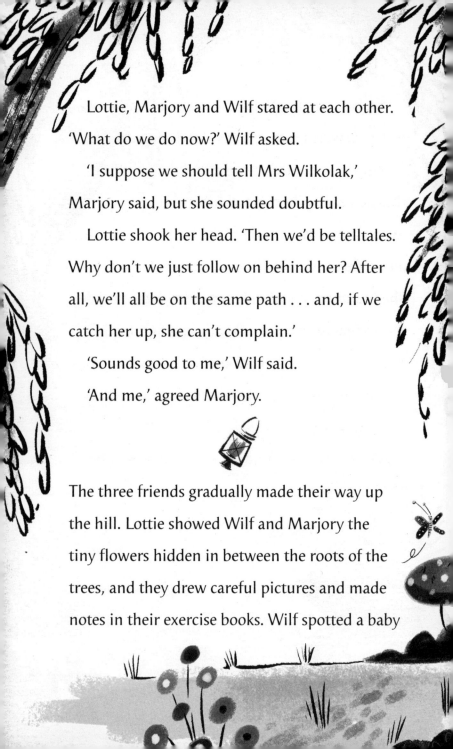

The three friends gradually made their way up the hill. Lottie showed Wilf and Marjory the tiny flowers hidden in between the roots of the trees, and they drew careful pictures and made notes in their exercise books. Wilf spotted a baby

rabbit crouched under
the bracken, and Marjory
found a woodmouse – and they
hugged each other in excitement
when they saw a roe deer and her
fawn sleeping peacefully in the dappled
shadows under a willow tree. They were
so fascinated that they completely forgot
about Aggie until they turned a corner,
and found her sitting on a log.

'You've been absolutely ages!' she complained. 'What on earth have you been doing?'

Lottie looked at her in surprise. 'I thought you wanted to be on your own!'

Aggie made a face. 'We're nearly at the top. Mr Sprinter will make a stupid fuss if I'm not with you lot.'

'Did you find any butterflies?' Marjory asked. 'We haven't.'

'I haven't seen a butterfly, but I've got LOADS of mushrooms and toadstools.' Aggie pointed at her backpack, which was bulging. 'Now hurry up! I'm starving! It'll all be ready. Mrs Sprinter makes the very best picnics.'

Aggie was right. When they came out of the woods at the top of the hill, Lottie was surprised to see that there was a wide expanse of grass

dotted with round boulders that made ideal seats and tables. Mrs Sprinter had spread a tablecloth over a wide, flat stone, and it was heaped with the most delicious-looking sandwiches. There were sausages sizzling on a barbecue, a massive bowl of soft brown and white rolls, a huge basket of shining red apples and a truly remarkable fruit cake.

Wilf, Marjory and Lottie stood and stared, but Aggie strode forward. 'Where are the plates?' she demanded. 'I'm ever so hungry! I'd like lots of cheese sandwiches, and about six sausages, please.'

Mrs Sprinter shook her head. 'We thought we'd wait until everyone gets here, Aggie. They won't be long . . . The little ones have already arrived, so we're just waiting for the rest of your class.'

Aggie looked annoyed, but she didn't dare say anything. She stomped away, and threw herself down on the grass.

Lottie was watching the chattering group of younger werewolves, and the more she looked, the more worried she felt. There was no sign of Larry.

'Can you spot Larry?' she asked Marjory. 'I know he was part of that group, but I can't see him.'

'I'm not sure,' Marjory said. 'Oh! Is that him rolling over and over? No . . . I don't think it is.'

'Come on,' Lottie said. 'Let's go and check.'

Wilf came to join them as they walked across the clearing. 'What's going on?'

'We can't find Larry,' Marjory told him. 'We're worried that he's gone missing.'

The little werewolves bounced up when they saw Wilf and the two older girls. 'Hello!'

'Is Larry here?' Lottie asked.

Dubby grinned at her. 'He's gone to find his red woolly hat, hasn't he, Tod?'

Tod nodded. 'He hooked it on to a tree when we was looking for bunny rabbits. He said he

didn't want it no more cos he was too hot
in his head—'

'But when we got here he said he did want it
after all.' Dubby made a face. 'He's a silly-billy.'

'Is the tree far away?' Wilf asked.

'Not far,' Tod told him. 'Larry said he'd be ever
so quick, didn't he, Dubby?'

'He said we wasn't to eat all the sausages
before he got back,' Dubby agreed.

Tod rubbed his nose. 'But he did look kind of
funny when he went.'

'What do you mean?' Wilf asked, but Tod
couldn't tell him.

'Just funny,' he said, and then, 'but not funny
ha ha. Funny like . . . like he was feeling funny.'

'Funny like a bunny,' Dubby added. He giggled
at his own joke, but for once Tod didn't join in.

'But he wasn't smiling, Dubs. Not at all.'

Marjory and Lottie looked at each other, but they had no time to discuss what Tod was trying to say. There was a flurry on the other side of the clearing, and Mr Sprinter came hurrying out of the woods. Mrs Wilkolak was with him, and so were the last few stragglers.

'Everybody here?' Mr Sprinter asked loudly. Then, without waiting for an answer, he said, 'Excellent! Let's eat . . . I'm starving!'

Before Lottie could say that Larry was missing, Mrs Sprinter had begun to hand out plates, and there was a mad rush towards the table. Lottie, Wilf and Marjory made their way to Mrs Wilkolak's side, but their teacher was deep in conversation with Mr Sprinter, and it was a few moments before she noticed the three of them

63

trying to attract her attention. 'Yes, my dears? What is it?'

'Larry's not here,' Lottie told her, 'and we're just a bit worried about him.'

Mrs Wilkolak's eyes sharpened. 'Not here? But wasn't he in the first group to reach the top of the hill?'

Marjory nodded. 'Yes, but Tod and Dubby say he went back to find his hat.'

'It's strange that I didn't meet him,' Mrs Wilkolak said slowly. 'If he came back down the path, I'd have bumped into him – and you can be certain I'd have sent him straight back. But Lottie – are you sure he's not hiding somewhere?

Waiting to jump out and give us all a fright?'

Lottie shook her head. 'I don't think so.' She paused, and then said, 'He was ever so worried about the fang fairy, so he wasn't in a very jokey mood.'

'What?' Her teacher stared at her. 'Goodness me, Lottie – why would he be worried about that? Everyone loves the fang fairy!'

Marjory, Wilf and Lottie looked at each other. What should they say? They didn't want to tell Mrs Wilkolak that Aggie had been making up scary stories and get her into trouble . . . but, if Larry really was missing, that was very serious.

'You know he's got a wobbly tooth,' Lottie said, 'well, he heard a story about it being a different fang fairy out here in the country . . . a nasty, fierce one.'

'And he thought she was trying to catch him,' Wilf added.

Mrs Wilkolak frowned. 'I'm not going to ask who told him such a silly story. Not now. We need to find him first.'

Lottie had been thinking. 'What if we went back down the path to look for him?' she suggested, and the teacher nodded.

'You're a sensible girl. Keep together and you won't come to any harm. Did his friends say where he left his hat?'

'Just that it wasn't very far away,' Lottie told her.

'Oh, dear.' Mrs Wilkolak sighed. 'I'll wait here

at the top of the path. Don't go into the woods! And let's keep our fingers crossed that you meet him bouncing up the hill, looking pleased with himself.'

CHAPTER SEVEN

'I hope they leave some of the picnic for us,' Wilf said as they began to make their way down the hill. 'My stomach keeps rumbling!'

'Mine too,' Lottie told him. 'Those sausages smelled amazing!'

Marjory gave a mock groan. 'Don't even talk about them. And that fruit cake! It looked utterly delicious!'

'There was an awful lot of food,' Wilf said hopefully. 'I'm sure there'll be something left.'

'Yes . . . all the mouldy old sandwiches that

nobody else wants.' Marjory made a face.

Lottie grinned at her. 'Poor us. There'll be
nothing but leftover crusts, and crumbs, and—'
She stopped mid-sentence. 'LOOK! Down there –
I can see something red! It's got to be Larry's hat!
And it's moving . . . He must be wearing it!'

Wilf and Marjory squinted in the direction
that she was pointing, but they couldn't
see anything.

'Quick! Go on ahead,' Wilf told her. 'You'll be
much faster than us!'

Lottie, with a gasp of excitement, began to run.
The trees and bushes were a green blur on either
side of her as she flew down the narrow path,
but her superpowers meant that she was hardly
out of breath when she reached the bright red
woolly hat . . .

Only to find that it was still hanging on a branch, and swinging to and fro in the breeze. There was no sign of Larry.

Her heart sinking, Lottie turned the hat over. She saw Larry's name . . . and then something else. A crumpled piece of paper was tucked inside. With trembling fingers, she straightened it out, and read the message written in large, crooked letters.

I gone hoMe.
I gone to find the nice fang fary.
My toof is very wobly.
LoVe Larry xx

'Oh, no . . .' Lottie stared at the paper. 'Oh, NO! Which way would he have gone?'

Wilf came hurrying up, followed by Marjory, and Lottie silently handed them the piece of paper.

'That's really bad,' Marjory said as she read it. 'Where can he be?'

'Anywhere.' Wilf frowned. 'Mrs Wilkolak would have seen him if he came this way, so he must have left the path somewhere higher up . . . but where? He wouldn't have the foggiest idea which way to go.'

'We need to tell her and Mr Sprinter,' Lottie said. She looked up at Jaws, who was circling overhead. 'Jaws . . . can you see any sign of Larry? The little cub you looked after last night? Could you fly over the trees and have a look around?'

The bat nodded, and flew off.

'Will he find him?' Marjory asked, but Lottie shook her head.

'Only if he's near here. Jaws doesn't like going too far away from me. Pa's always telling him he mustn't leave me on my own unless it's an emergency. Come on . . . we've got to tell the grown-ups!'

Larry's note caused a sensation. Mr Sprinter went very pale, and Mrs Wilkolak and Mrs Sprinter looked really worried. 'We need to search the hill immediately,' Mrs Sprinter said. 'There's that dreadfully dangerous cliff!'

'And the river,' Mrs Wilkolak added. 'It's very fast-flowing, and I'm sure Larry can't swim.'

'He doesn't like water, Mrs Wilkolak,' Tod said. He and Dubby were both unusually subdued and, for a brief moment, Lottie wondered if they knew more than they were admitting to.

'We'll split up,' Mr Sprinter announced. 'The younger ones must stay here with you, Mrs Sprinter, but we'll divide the older ones into three groups. Aggie, Lottie, Wilf and Marjory – you'll be in the first group. I'm going to send you four without a teacher, so please watch where you're going. I'd like you to keep to the upper slopes of the hill. Check behind those trees, then come straight back and report to Mrs Sprinter. I'm almost certain Larry will have stayed near the path, but you may as well go and look.'

Lottie nodded. 'We'll be very careful.'

Aggie was digging in her backpack. 'I've got a pair of simply amazing binoculars, and lots of rope. I'm prepared for anything.'

'Let's hope the rope won't be needed,' Mr Sprinter said. He glanced up at the sky, and a worried look came over his face. 'We need to hurry. Those clouds look suspiciously like rain to me . . . and the last thing we want is for everyone to get soaked.'

'I've got the best raincoat ever!' Aggie dived into her pack again, and pulled out a bright yellow macintosh. 'I knew it would come in

useful. I don't suppose anyone else thought to bring one.' She put it on, and looked pleased with herself. 'I expect you'll want me to be in charge of our group, Mr Sprinter. I'm all ready!'

Wilf nudged Lottie. 'Typical,' he whispered.

Aggie heard him, and scowled. 'I'm the oldest, and I know this hill really well.'

'It doesn't really matter who's the leader,' Lottie told her. 'The important thing is to find Larry.'

'Of course it is. Don't you think I know that?' Aggie looked superior. 'So we should stop arguing, and hurry up and get going!' She swung her pack on to her back, and marched away without looking to see if Lottie, Wilf and Marjory were following.

Lottie stayed behind for a moment. 'If we

75

see anything, I'll send Jaws with a message,' she promised, and Mrs Wilkolak smiled at her.

'That's an excellent thought, Lottie. Thank you.'

CHAPTER EIGHT

By the time Lottie had caught up with Aggie, Wilf and Marjory, the wind was getting up, and the clouds were beginning to cover the sun. She tried not to shiver as she walked along, looking carefully left and right as she went. Jaws hadn't seen any sign of Larry, so now he was sitting on Lottie's shoulder, hoping he wasn't going to get wet. He snuggled closer to her ear, and shut his eyes.

'We must be sure to look everywhere,' Aggie announced. 'So no talking!'

Wilf snorted loudly. 'Don't be silly. We've got to work together. What if one of us notices something? We'll have to talk to each other then.'

Aggie stuck her nose in the air. 'It's you that's silly, Wilf. I'll find Larry easily.' She pulled her binoculars out and waved them in the air. 'I can see absolutely everything through these. I'm like an eagle. As soon as we're on the other side of those trees, I'll be able to look down the hill, and then I'm sure to spot him. And, what's more, I'm going to tell him what a silly little cub he is!'

Lottie had been trying her best not to lose her temper, but this was too much for her. 'Don't be so horrid, Aggie! If you hadn't told him that scary story, he wouldn't have run away!'

'I'm NOT horrid!' Aggie was trembling with

anger. 'And it was a funny story, not a scary one! I don't see why everyone made such a fuss about it ... If a spoilt little cub took it seriously, that's not my fault!'

'Yes it is!' Lottie was just as angry as Aggie. 'And I think it was you who made those claw marks round Larry's tent! You wanted to scare him even more, and that's as mean as mean can be!'

'That's SUCH a lie!' Aggie stamped her foot. 'I'm not going to stay and listen to you, Lottie Luna! You think you're so smart and clever and better than anyone else, but you're not – you're just rubbish!' And, before Lottie could say another word, Aggie had stormed away between the trees.

'Oooops.' Lottie bit her lip. 'Maybe I shouldn't have said that.'

Marjory took her arm. 'Yes you should,' she said, and Wilf nodded.

Lottie smiled at her friends, but she was feeling very uncomfortable. She had no way of proving that it was Aggie who had made the claw marks; it might easily have been Tod and Dubby, or even someone else entirely.

'We'd better go after her. We really shouldn't split up. We're meant to be the sensible ones, and – much more importantly – we're meant to be looking for Larry!'

Wilf sighed. 'You're right. Come on, then.'

It was easy to tell which way Aggie had gone in

between the trees as the ground was damp, and her footprints were clear.

'We can track her,' Wilf said, but Lottie was staring at a second set of prints.

'Look!' she said. 'Little footprints! They look like boots . . . and they're quite fresh. Do you think they're Larry's?'

Marjory came to inspect them. 'I'd say so. I noticed that he was wearing boots and these look just about the right size.'

Lottie's eyes shone. 'Brilliant! Let's get going! Maybe Aggie's already found him! Won't she be pleased if she has?' And she hurried forward, Wilf and Marjory close behind her.

It was dark under the thick canopy of leaves, and curtains of ivy hung from the twisted branches. The ground was damp and spongy, and brambles caught at their clothes, and held them back. It felt quite different from the sunny woods they had walked through on their way to the top

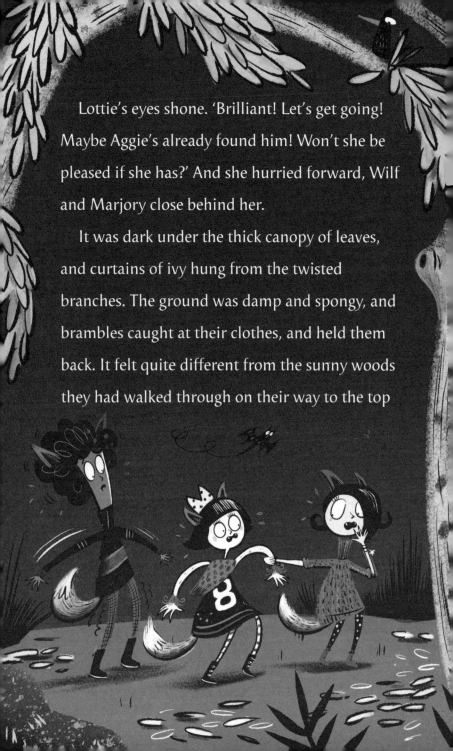

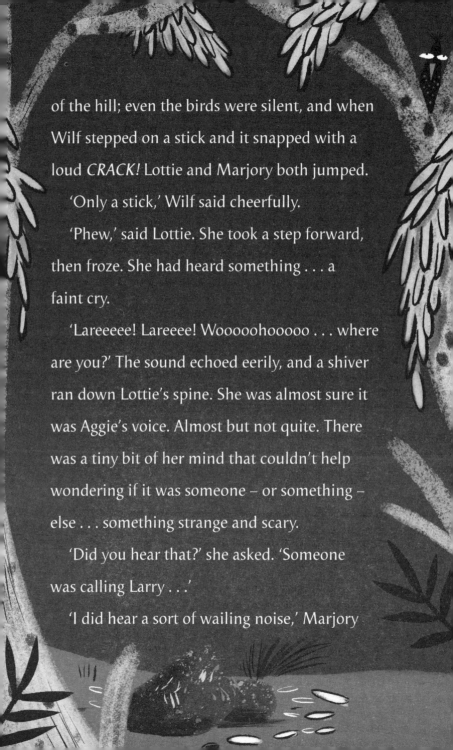

of the hill; even the birds were silent, and when Wilf stepped on a stick and it snapped with a loud *CRACK!* Lottie and Marjory both jumped.

'Only a stick,' Wilf said cheerfully.

'Phew,' said Lottie. She took a step forward, then froze. She had heard something . . . a faint cry.

'Lareeeee! Lareeee! Wooooohooooo . . . where are you?' The sound echoed eerily, and a shiver ran down Lottie's spine. She was almost sure it was Aggie's voice. Almost but not quite. There was a tiny bit of her mind that couldn't help wondering if it was someone – or something – else . . . something strange and scary.

'Did you hear that?' she asked. 'Someone was calling Larry . . .'

'I did hear a sort of wailing noise,' Marjory

said, and she blushed. 'I wasn't going to say anything, because I thought I might be imagining it – but it sounded spooky, like Aggie's horrid fang fairy!'

Lottie grinned at her. 'I thought that too!'

'Of course it was Aggie.' Wilf was matter-of-fact. 'Who else would it be? But if you two were scared by it just imagine what poor little Larry must be thinking! Come on. Let's hurry!'

But there was no sign of either Aggie or Larry when the three friends emerged from the darkness of the trees. In front of them was a steep slope covered in purple heather and dotted with large, jagged rocks, and down below they could hear the sound of rushing water. The clouds overhead were grey and heavy, and a mist was rising from the river. The bottom of the hill was

swathed in wisps of fog that half hid the trees that grew there.

'Oh, no! Now we've lost Aggie as well as Larry,' Marjory said. 'What should we do?'

'We're going to find them both.' Lottie sounded very determined. 'If they've gone down that slope, they'll be in danger.'

Wilf nodded. 'There's a sheer drop between here and the river, and there's a marsh as well. Mr Sprinter warned us about it last year.'

'That's why we're supposed to stay up at the top of the hill.' Marjory was frowning. 'I'd have thought Aggie would have known that.'

Lottie didn't answer – she was staring around. Where could Aggie and Larry have gone? Even with her amazing eyesight, she could see no clues. It was as if they'd vanished into nothingness. She

rubbed her eyes, and looked again . . . and this time something caught her attention. There was a patch of trampled grass by one of the largest rocks, and she was almost sure she could see a piece of paper on the ground.

'Someone's been down there,' she said. 'We ought to see if there are any clues, or more footprints. I'll go and look.' She hesitated. 'I'm not being bossy . . . it's just that I'm a bit quicker than you two. If there's anything important, I'll wave!'

Wilf grinned at her. 'It's okay, Lottie.'

Marjory nodded. 'We know all about your secret powers, Lottie Luna! And you're not just a bit quicker than us – you're loads quicker!'

Lottie gave them a beaming smile. It was wonderful having friends who understood, and

who didn't make a big fuss. Then, being careful not to slip, she ran down the slope.

When she got to the bottom, Lottie could see that she was right about a clue. Not only had the grass been trampled, but there were small footprints in a patch of mud beneath the rock, and the piece of paper was a loose page from Larry's notebook. There was a picture of a bird on it, but no helpful message. All it said was:

She waved up at Marjory and Wilf, and they came sliding down to join her.

'Larry was definitely here,' she told them. She went round the rock, and there, on the other side, were larger footprints.

'Aggie!' Lottie stared in surprise. It looked exactly as if Larry had been on one side of the rock, and Aggie on the other . . . but why? Why weren't they together?

A thought came to Lottie, and she swung back round the rock. 'Marjory,' she said, 'your feet are smaller than mine . . . could you stand in Larry's footprints?'

Marjory looked surprised, and she tried to do as Lottie asked, but she couldn't until she crouched right down underneath the rock.

'Wow!' She wriggled out again. 'What was he doing under there?'

'I think,' Lottie said slowly, 'that he was hiding—'

'From the fang fairy!' Wilf interrupted her. 'I bet Aggie had terrified him out of his wits!'

'We don't actually know that.' Lottie was trying hard to be fair. 'She might have been here before or after him.'

'That's right,' Marjory agreed. 'I think she genuinely wanted to find Larry . . . She's not completely awful.'

'The footprints look very fresh.' Lottie stood up. 'They can't be far away. They could be behind any of those rocks . . . or maybe they're in among those trees at the bottom of the slope?' She stared down the hill, hoping she might be able to see even the tiniest sign that Aggie and

Larry had gone that way, but even with her amazing eyesight she couldn't find anything out of the ordinary.

'Rocks . . . grass . . . rushes . . . willow trees . . . oh! Bother that mist! I can't see anything further – hang on a moment!' Lottie concentrated even harder. 'If there are rushes, the ground must be marshy . . . Oh, dear. That's dangerous!' An idea came to her, and she tickled Jaws under his chin.

He was asleep on her shoulder, but the tickling woke him, and he yawned and stretched.

'Eeeek?'

'Jaws,' Lottie said, 'could you fly around and see if you can see any sign of Aggie or Larry? Behind the rocks?'

Jaws yawned, stretched his wings and did as he was asked. Up he flew, and circled a couple of times before suddenly squeaking loudly and dropping back down.

'Did you see Larry?' Lottie asked eagerly, but Jaws shook his head. 'Oh . . . was it Aggie?' This time Jaws nodded, and pointed urgently with a wing.

'What was she doing?' Wilf asked.

Jaws squeaked an answer he couldn't understand. Lottie, however, gasped.

'Aggie's in trouble! We've got to find her – she's somewhere near those willows . . . and it's

marshland down there!'

And she began to run. Wilf and Marjory chased after her, avoiding the jagged rocks as best they could. As they ran, they heard a frantic shout.

'Help! Somebody help me! I'm sinking!'

CHAPTER NINE

Lottie was the first to see Aggie. She was up to her knees in thick mud, and sinking fast. She couldn't move forwards or backwards because, every time she tried, she sank a little deeper. When she saw Lottie running towards her, she shrieked, 'Help me! Help me! I saw Larry and I was chasing after him . . . but I didn't see it was horrible, beastly mud and now I'm going to drooooooown!'

'No you're not,' Lottie said. Without a second thought, she plunged in and waded towards

Aggie, her hands outstretched. Her extra strength meant she was able to move easily, and she gave Aggie an anxious glance; would Aggie notice how strong she was? But Aggie was much too scared to notice anything. Tears were streaming down her face, and she was sobbing hysterically.

As Lottie reached her, Aggie grabbed on to Lottie so hard that she almost pulled her over.

Lottie, with an effort, managed to stay upright, and with a loud *SQUELCH!* she pulled Aggie free. A couple of minutes later, they were back on dry land, and Aggie immediately collapsed in a hiccuping heap in front of Wilf and Marjory.

Lottie knelt down in front of her and handed her a hankie so she could wipe the mud and tears off her face. 'Aggie! You said you were chasing Larry! Which way did he go?'

'I wasn't chasing him.' Aggie was beginning to recover. 'I was chasing after him . . . That's different! I saw him running in among those willow trees, and I tried to take a short cut and that's when I ended up in that horrible bog – atchoo!' She sneezed loudly. 'I want to go back to the camp! I want to go right NOW! I'm covered in mud and I'm cold and wet. If I don't get warm

95

and dry, I just know I'll get a terrible cold!'

Lottie stood up. 'We can't go back yet. We've got to look for Larry. He could be in danger. Which way did he go?'

'I told you! He ran into the trees,' Aggie said. 'But I can't go any further . . . I really can't!' She gave a loud, self-pitying groan. 'Mummy always says I catch cold ever so easily. I need to go back!'

'Aggie!' Lottie lost her temper. She stamped her foot, and water squelched out of her shoe. 'Don't you ever think of anyone but yourself? A poor little werewolf cub is lost all because of your silly story and now you're worrying about catching a cold?'

Aggie blinked. 'I did try to find Larry!'

'But you didn't!' Lottie's eyes were blazing. 'And, if anything bad has happened to him, it'll

be your fault! Now we're going to find him, and we're all going to go together!'

'I'm coming!' Wilf leaped forward.

'Me too,' said Marjory, but Aggie began to wail again.

'My shoes are full of mud, and I'm frozen, and I'm soaking wet . . . PLEASE don't make me go any further!' She pushed her backpack into Lottie's arms. 'Here! You can have all the things I've collected . . . and my binoculars . . . and the rope. Let me stay here . . . please!'

Lottie frowned. 'We can't leave you on your own, Aggie. It's not safe. You'll have to come with us.'

'Just a minute.' Marjory looked at the muddy and miserable girl, and shook her head. 'Lottie, you and Wilf go on ahead. I'll follow with Aggie.

She's not going to be much help the way she is . . .
She'll only hold you back.'

Lottie flung her arms round Marjory, and
gave her a massive hug. 'You're the kindest, most
thoughtful person I've ever met,' she said, 'and
I really wish you were coming with us. It's so
much nicer when it's the three of us together.'
She glared at Aggie before striding away,
followed by Wilf.

Skirting carefully round the marsh, they soon
reached the weeping willow trees, and Lottie
stopped and stood very still.

'What are you doing?' Wilf asked.

'Listening,' Lottie told him. 'If Larry's here
and walking around, I'll hear him because the

ground's covered in dry leaves.' She shut her eyes, and Wilf waited patiently while she concentrated. When she opened her eyes again, she looked worried. 'I definitely heard him,' she said. 'I heard him running – but then all of a sudden it was quiet. Oh, Wilf! Could he have fallen in the river?' Lottie went pale at the thought.

'Did you hear a splash?' Wilf asked.

'No . . . and I would have, wouldn't I?' Lottie agreed. 'But at least we know which way to go. He was over there.' She pointed.

The two friends fought their way in between the close-growing bushes and twisted willows. Lottie kept in front of Wilf to try clear some kind of a path, but even with her extra strength it wasn't easy. Jaws flitted in and out of the undergrowth, being careful to keep close to her;

he was aware that she was struggling, and he could see that her necklace was as dull as he had ever seen it. She was obviously very anxious, and that made him anxious too.

'Look!' Lottie pointed at the ground. 'A footprint! A little one!' She redoubled her efforts, pushing her way through the tangle of drooping willow branches until at last she and Wilf burst out into the open – and she clutched at Wilf's arm.

'STOP!'

They were balanced on the very edge of a steep drop. Below them a furious river rushed and tumbled over jagged rocks, and spray flew

so high in the air that Lottie could feel it on her face. Cautiously, she and Wilf peered over the edge . . .

And there was Larry.

CHAPTER TEN

The little werewolf cub was
clinging to the knotted roots
of a gnarled old willow
that was growing out of a
crack halfway down the
cliff. His eyes were tightly

shut and he was trembling all over. Lottie was
frightened that if she called out to him she might
shock him into letting go. Instead, she began to
whistle 'We're All Going on a Jolly Howlyday',
softly at first, then growing louder. Wilf joined
in, and Larry's eyelids flickered . . . and he opened
his eyes.

'Lottie!' he whispered. 'Help me!'

'Keep very still,' Lottie warned him. 'I'm here
with Wilf, and we're going to rescue you.' She
turned to Wilf, and whispered, 'He's awfully far
down. Even if I can find a way to reach him, I'm
not sure how I'll bring him up with me . . . OH!
How could I have forgotten?' Swinging Aggie's
backpack on to the ground, she unzipped it. 'Here
it is! Aggie's rope!' And she pulled it out with
a triumphant shout. Running to the strongest-

looking tree, Lottie tied one end round the trunk, and knotted it tightly. The other end she threw over the cliff and then paused.

'Wilf, can you pull Larry on to the grass when I get him back up again?'

'I'm ready,' Wilf said, and Lottie held on to the rope and climbed over the edge of the cliff. Bit by bit, she climbed steadily down, while Larry watched her anxiously, and Wilf held his breath. At last she was level with Larry, and he gave a loud squeak of excitement – and, before she could tell him what to do next, he had launched himself at her. Grabbing Lottie's arm, he held on tightly.

'I knowed you'd save me, Lottie! I knowed it!'

But there was a problem. Larry wouldn't climb on to Lottie's back, and he wouldn't hang round her neck. He was much too scared. He

whimpered and cried, and wouldn't let go of her
arm – and that meant she only had one arm to
hold the rope.

Up above, Wilf heaved as hard as he could,
but he wasn't strong enough to pull Lottie and
little Larry up together. To make matters worse,
it was beginning to rain, and the rope was
growing slippery.

Lottie's heart was beating fast. How could
she save Larry? Her mind whirled as she tried to

think of a way to get the two of them to the top
of the cliff. Jaws was circling anxiously round and
round, and Lottie called to him, 'Jaws! Fly back!
Get help!'

And the little bat flew away as fast as he could.

Lottie was getting colder and wetter by the
second, and she began to worry that she wouldn't
be able to hold on to the rope much longer.
Her fingers were getting painfully numb – she
absolutely had to make a decision. Should she
hang on, and hope that help came, or should
she take action?

Lottie took a deep breath. *I'm Lottie Luna,* she
told herself. *I can do this!* And she made up her
mind. 'Larry, I'm going to try to climb the cliff
again. Shut your eyes very tightly, and hang on.'

She took a deep breath, twisted the rope round

her feet, and pulled herself up a few centimetres. Then, hanging on with one arm, she managed to slide her feet up enough so she could move again. Slowly, agonisingly slowly, she managed to haul herself and Larry up the cliff inch by painful inch. Her arms began to ache, and Larry felt heavier by the minute . . . and the rope grew more and more slippery.

Not much further, she told herself. *Only another metre or so . . .*

CHAPTER ELEVEN

There was a tug on the rope. Not just a tug, but a heave . . . and the heave was followed by another, and then another. Lottie found herself sailing upwards, and Larry gave a squeal of delight.

'Wilf!' he yelled. 'It's Wilf and Marjory! Oh . . .' His smile faded as he was hauled over the edge of the cliff and safely on to the grass. 'And Aggie . . .'

Lottie came next. She scrambled up after Larry, and beamed at Wilf and Marjory. 'I'm SO pleased

to see you!' And she hugged them tightly.

Aggie was standing to one side, and Marjory gave Lottie a gentle nudge. 'It took all three of us to pull you both to the top,' she said. 'Aggie helped . . . she helped a lot.'

'Well, I say a HUGE thank you to all of you!' Lottie said, and she gave Aggie a grateful smile.

'I honestly thought I was going to have to let go of the rope because my arms were hurting SO much! I'm sure they're twice as long as they used to be.' She made a face. 'They still hurt.'

'Eeeek!' There was a flapping of wings, and Jaws came fluttering down. When he saw Lottie was safe, he looped a celebratory loop, then settled on her shoulder. 'Eeeeek,' he said again, and Lottie smiled.

'You led the teachers here? Well done, Jaws!'

She had hardly finished speaking when the willow branches were swept aside and Mrs Wilkolak appeared, puffing hard.

'Lottie! Larry! Wilf! Marjory! Aggie! Thank goodness you're all safe!'

Lottie had never seen her teacher look so anxious. 'We're fine,'

she said. 'Well, my arms hurt a bit, but that's all.'

Larry pushed in front of her. 'Lottie did rescue me!' he announced. 'The horrid fang fairy was calling me and I runned away and fell off the cliff, but Lottie – she comed down for me on a rope.'

'I see,' Mrs Wilkolak said, and she turned and looked thoughtfully at Aggie. 'Would this fang-fairy nonsense have something to do with you, Aggie?'

Aggie stared at the ground, and Lottie saw that tears were dripping off the end of her nose. She was shivering miserably as she said, 'Yes.'

'Aggie told a bad story!' Larry was delighted to see her looking so unhappy. 'She said the horrid fang fairy would get me and she chased me and she—'

'Just a minute, Larry.' Lottie put her arm round the little cub. 'Aggie might have told you a horrid story, but she didn't chase you to scare you – she was trying to help you. And –' she turned to her teacher – 'I wouldn't have been able to rescue Larry if Aggie hadn't had the sense to bring a rope, Mrs Wilkolak.'

'Also we needed Aggie's help to pull Lottie and Larry up the cliff,' Marjory added. 'We couldn't have done it without her. Truly!'

There was a long pause, and then Aggie whispered, 'I'm sorry. I really am. I did tell Larry the story, but I promise I didn't chase him! I

was feeling bad that he'd run away, so I really, REALLY wanted to be the one to find him. I ran after him, and I called him . . . but he wouldn't listen . . . ATCHOOOOO!'

'Hmm.' Mrs Wilkolak considered Aggie for a moment. 'It sounds like you might be getting a cold. I suggest that I go back with you to the camp to collect your things, Aggie, and then someone will take you home. It seems to me that you have had punishment enough . . . and you do seem to have redeemed yourself a little at the end. As for the rest of you –' she smiled at Lottie and her friends – 'hurry back to the top of the hill, and take Larry with you. There's still a huge amount of food left . . . and you must be very hungry!'

'Starving,' Wilf said, and Larry giggled.

'Me too! I want sausages!'

113

When Lottie, Wilf, Marjory and Larry reached the top of the hill, they were met with a huge cheer. Mrs Sprinter relit the barbecue, and minutes later sausages were sizzling cheerfully ... and Larry was sitting with his friends, telling them his adventures, and boasting about how brave he'd been.

Lottie, listening while she tucked into a

plateful of sandwiches, smiled at Marjory.

'So all's well that ends well,' she said.

Marjory nodded. 'We sorted out a lot of things, but I do still wonder who made those claw marks. Aggie owned up to everything else . . . but not that.'

Wilf pointed at Tod and Dubby. 'I'd say it was those two.' He strode over to the group of little cubs, and bent down to talk to them. A moment later, he was back, grinning. 'I was right. But they

won't be playing a trick like that again. It really
worried them when Larry ran away. They thought
it was all their fault.'

There was a sudden loud shriek. 'LOTTIE!' It
was Larry. 'Lottie – look! My tooth! It comed out!
It comed out in a sausage!'

'Hurrah!' Lottie gave him a thumbs up. 'We'll
have to have a celebration party round the
campfire tonight!'

Mr Sprinter heard her, and nodded. 'Indeed we will. And I think you should take your tooth home with you, and put it under your pillow when you're in your own bed. That way you can be certain it's the right fang fairy.'

'Good idea,' Lottie said.

Larry put his head on one side. 'I'll put it under my pillow tonight to keep it safe,' he said. 'Just in case the nice one knows where to come.'

Mr Sprinter shook his head. 'Don't count on it, Larry.'

CHAPTER TWELVE

Tooth Party was a wild success. The rain clouds had blown away, and it was a lovely evening. The campfire burned brightly as all the werewolves sang songs and told very cheerful stories . . . and the hot chocolate, according to Marjory, was the best ever. Mrs Sprinter cooked slice after slice of pizza, each one covered in golden bubbling cheese, and everyone ate so much they could hardly move.

Lottie, sitting with Wilf and Marjory, sighed happily. 'I just love camping,' she said. 'Especially

with my very best friends. It's the most wonderful thing ever! Do you know, I'm having such a fabulous time that I actually feel sorry for Aggie having to go home with a cold.'

'Well, I don't,' Wilf said. 'Well . . . not too much anyway.'

They all laughed and Lottie's moonstone necklace gleamed as brightly as the stars up above in the deep blue evening sky. Jaws saw it shining, and was happy. He knew King Lupo would ask him if Lottie had been suitably dignified and princessy . . . and he was going to answer, YES! YES! YES!

All too soon, Mrs Wilkolak was telling the happy campers that it was time for bed. They

119

packed up the supper things, and then Mr
Sprinter put out the campfire while Mrs Sprinter
and Mrs Wilkolak did the dishes.

Wilf, Marjory and Lottie couldn't stop yawning
as they washed their faces and brushed their
teeth.

'Who would have thought camping could be
so exciting?' Marjory said as they crawled into
their sleeping bags.

'I know.' Wilf shook his head. 'I think it must
be something to do with Lottie! She makes
everything special—'

'OOOOOOOOOOH!'

Wilf was interrupted by a wild shriek of joy
from the tent next door, and he, Marjory and

Lottie leaped out bed and rushed to see what had happened. They found Larry waving a silver coin, and smiling from ear to ear.

'It's the fang fairy! She's been! I got a silver coin under my pillow! I really, really have!' Larry was ecstatic. 'You was right, Lottie! She's a very, very, VERY good fang fairy and I LOVE her!'

'WOW!' Lottie's eyes opened wide. 'That's wonderful, Larry!' And she tucked the excited little cub back into bed. 'Now, sleep well . . . and sweet dreams!'

As the three friends wriggled back into their sleeping bags, Marjory looked at Wilf and Lottie. 'Isn't that lovely! Where could the coin have come from?'

Lottie shook her head. 'Who knows?'

Wilf yawned. 'Do you think it could have been Aggie who put the silver coin under Larry's pillow? To say she was sorry?'

'Maybe.' Marjory rubbed her eyes. 'The great thing is that Larry's happy and not scared any more. Night-night . . .'

'Night-night.' Wilf yawned again. 'See you in the morning!'

Lottie snuggled down, cosy and warm, and smiled to herself.

Actually, there's only one person who could have put it there, she thought sleepily. The fang fairy!

LOOK OUT FOR LOTTIE LUNA'S NEXT ADVENTURE

COMING SOON ...

LOTTIE LUNA

AND THE GIANT GARGOYLE

HAVE YOU READ LOTTIE LUNA'S FIRST ADVENTURE?

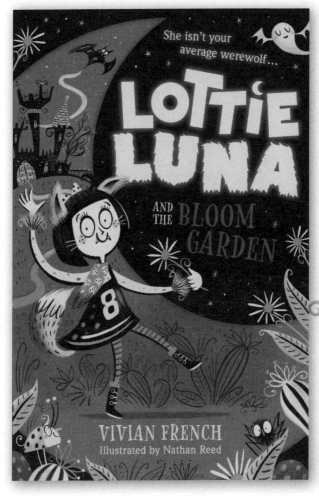

She isn't your average werewolf...

LOTTIE LUNA

AND THE BLOOM GARDEN

VIVIAN FRENCH

Illustrated by Nathan Reed

HAVE YOU READ
LOTTIE LUNA'S SECOND
ADVENTURE?

She isn't your
average werewolf...

LOTTIE LUNA

AND THE TWILIGHT PARTY

VIVIAN FRENCH

Illustrated by Nathan Reed